FEARNE COTTON

Hungry Babies

Illustrated by SHEENA DEMPSEY

ANDERSEN PRESS

We're the Hungry Babies,
look what we can eat:
fruit and veg, milk and bread,
sometimes a little treat.

Rex eats toast for breakfast.
Today he wants to share –
Bingo can't believe his luck,
what a naughty pair!

Honey likes to feed herself.
Oh dear, what a mess!
Food on her face and in her hair,
and down her pretty dress.

Poor Emily's unwell today,
wants cuddles from her mum.
No nursery or food for her –
she's got a poorly tum.

Prakash is at the market,
helping Granny shop:
fresh fruit in the basket
and mango down his top.

We're the Hungry Babies
waiting for our lunch.
Kit likes to eat bananas –
"Don't eat that whole bunch!"

Sophie loves a picnic,
her lunch spread on a rug.
Sandwiches and strawberries,
and juice drunk from a mug.

Today is Maya's birthday.
She's going out to eat.

Please
WAIT
to be
SEATED

But Jack is so annoying,
and won't stay in his seat.

He runs around the restaurant,
makes bubbles with his straw,

hits Maya with his menu,
spills juice all on the floor!

Then the fish and chips arrive
and Jack eats all his food.
Maya's birthday treat is fun
(but that burp from Jack was rude).

George likes cheese on everything:
his pasta and his bread,
his yogurt and his jelly,
and sometimes on his head!

Winnie's in the kitchen,
helping Daddy bake:
sausage rolls for teatime
and a giant chocolate cake.

We're the Hungry Babies.
"Snack time now," says Mum.
"Yuk!" says Tom. "Don't like it."
Sam says, "Yummy yum."

It's birthday tea at Maya's house,
all her friends have come.
There's lots of food for everyone
and leftovers for Mum.

Yes we're the Hungry Babies,
from morning through to night.
With milk to drink at bedtime
as we cuddle up so tight.